SOLDIER BOY

BY TOM NORTH

1

Kevin

There I was. Week five in the middle of butt-fuck nowhere. I don't think I'd ever been so consistently thirsty in my entire fucking life. Every day, all day, my mouth was as dry as a camel's pussy. I'd give anything for a suck on an ice pole. Me and the lads spent a lot of summers as kids just sat around on our bikes on any bit of green we could find; eating ice poles and shouting at anyone stupid enough to walk by us. We were complete nob ends; it's true, but it was good fun at the time at least. In fact right at that moment, it seemed like that was the best time of my life. But any time of my life was better than this.

It was five weeks since our posting there in the middle of a dessert and absolutely no action to speak of. None. Not even a wild dog to fend off. Just endless sun beating down on us and the odd mirage of a naked beauty coming into view on the horizon; only to find it was one of the scouts coming back from endless patrol of the empty territory around us.

Don't know how many lads were posted there exactly. Maybe one hundred, hard to be sure. With our skins-heads and identical sand brown camos it was hard to actually distinguish us as individual people. Just a bunch of dried up prunes burning in the heat.

I was so excited to finally get there, all them years in training, dreaming of finally getting into the action and doing some good in the world. Something to make all that boredom and bullshit to get there, worth it. But no, just more boredom and bullshit. Only less women; and less rain.

They flew us into this camp cause there was some intel of a rogue militia group nearby that were planning an attack on a local town. I don't know if the intel was dodgy or if they just needed to make up an excuse to make us look busy. But there was certainly no sign of any attack any time soon.

The boys were all going feral. Bored out of their fucking brains and horny as hell with nothing to do with it. The amount of bust-ups over home-brew beer was unreal. They all needed a good night out and a good woman to spend the night with. Cheer 'em up and takes their minds off it. Or at least something to shoot.

Most of 'em came from small towns; they'd never seen more action than a weekend brawl at a local pub. Some old uncle getting too twatted and ending his night getting decked by someone more in his peak. I felt sorry for 'em all. They were even younger than me; and even more hopeful. Ain't easy being a bloke these days. Feels like we're getting blamed for everything; but we're as lost as anyone else. I mean, we must be. Who would choose to go into the field of combat if he was completely happy with his lot. We knew we were just there to fight for someone else's oil. But what else were we supposed to do? Spend our lives flipping burgers to fill someone else's wallet? At least this way we get to pretend we're heroes. Pretend that something still means anything. We knew the truth though. Well, some of us did.

I'd not killed anyone yet, not even had the chance. I didn't know what it would feel like. Maybe I would feel like a hero. Protecting Queen and country. I hoped so.

Mum was livid when I told her I was coming, "You're throwing you bloody life away you stupid little twerp. You wanna waste your life? Go get someone pregnant. It's better than getting yourself killed!" No chance of getting killed there though. Unless I was dying of thirst; or boredom. She'll be alright, I thought, once she sees how much stronger and better I am after being in the field. She'll soon change her mind. Or not; I don't suppose it really matters either way. But I did for once in my life, want to make the stupid cow proud of me.

I remember in school when I got sent home for punching this lad in the eye; she looked so disappointed in me. Like I was a piece of shit on her shoe. I always felt like I somehow had to make it up to her for that. Well, for all the times she gave me that look; just once I wanted to see her look at me the way she looked at my sister. She never even did much special, she got pregnant at fifteen. But now she got a supervisor role in the local Primark and I've never seen my mum look more proud in my life. Fuck, if that's all it takes, why can't she give that look to me? I don't know. Maybe I'm that bad.

Don't suppose she'd even noticed I was gone to be honest. Don't suppose anyone had. It was just her and my sister back home. No girlfriend to speak of, and just a few mates dotted about. I did think of staying for this one girl, Dilly; beautiful she was, but bloody hell she wanted to move fast. Wanted me to move in after two months. I couldn't handle it. Not ready to play Mr & Mrs. I've seen that. Drove my Dad up the wall - no wonder he left.

I'd been sat on a crate of freeze-dried fucking carrots for about an hour. Top wrapped round my waist, letting the sweat drip down me as the sun browned me off like a bloody bourbon. All I could do was smoke to pass the time, I did't even like smoking, there was just bugger all else to do. Sit, smoke, think about what a stupid decision it was to come here.

Couple of the lads were playing a game of footie. But it's too hot if you ask me. Sam's always up for a game. He comes rocking into the tent like he's been snorting coke, looking wired as a fucking hyena, "Come on man, just a kick about. I need to burn my juices of. If I can't fuck at least I can pummel the ball". Lovely bloody image. I let him get on with it. He's roped in Dave and Tony, a couple of blokes with more muscle than brain. Could probably talk 'em into to just about anything if you had more than a few words in your vocabulary.

Last week I convinced 'em to nick some cigarettes from the boys in the tent one over from us. Managed to nick a whole box of 'em. I stashed about twenty packets in my stuff before the lads cottoned on and had a big bust up. Nice to have some boys to do the dirty work for you.

Anyway, there they were kicking about their ball, soaking bloody wet from perspiration, panting like dogs and looking just as dumb. Then all of of a sudden Sam pelts the ball like a madman, sending it flying at full force into Tony's wet forehead. It slaps into him and sends silence like a bullet round the camp. Tony staggers a bit, looks a bit dumbfounded then collapses like a sack of rice, bam, straight into the floor sending a little clouds of dust sprinkling the air around him. I couldn't even be bothered to move. I was just fascinated by the whole spectacle of it. The sight of this tonne of bricks hitting the ground so hard, being taken down by the skinny little twerp. It was like David and Goliath, but less spectacular.

Sam fretted; running over to him like a concerned mother flapping his hands about. Dave was still taking the time to process what had happened, his thick skull moving as fast as an oil spill, getting stuck on reality.

Then, out he trots, lieutenant stick up his arse, Mason. Not much older than any of us, but he'd been bumped up the chain a bit faster cause he'd been to uni. Don't even know what he studied, probably fine art or some shit. But anyway, here he was somehow above the likes of a normal squaddie and taking every opportunity to flex a bit of power. He didn't know what he was doing with himself, the prat.

"Boys! Get a stretcher from the Med tent immediately! Man down!" He squawked at them.

"He's fine Sir, just a bash to the head from a football. He'll come round in a second." Sam fired back.

"I said get to the med tent. I've seen stuff like this before, an innocent bash to the head the next minute he's fitting and gushing blood from his eyes."

I don't know what Hollywood fluff he'd been watching to get that idea. But there was no arguing with the chain of command. Off Sam trotted like an obedient little puppy. He came back a few minutes late with a couple of lads in tow and a stretcher, just as promised. Skinny young things though, the lot of them. Don't know how they thought they'd get that lump up there. One of the lads I recognised. Young Welsh guy with a little too much tub around the middle and little too much to prove. The other lad though, Indian looking fella. Never seen him before, he somehow managed to keep some hair on his head, dark black. Wavy. He looked like he knew exactly what he was doing, like he'd seen more than half of these lads combined. Don't know where he'd come from. For some reason I couldn't stop myself from staring at him.

He knelt on the floor next to Tony and tried to roll him onto the stretcher, all three of them huffing and struggling like stuck pigs. Don't know how there was someone about the place I didn't know. Weren't many of us here. But then again, I suppose I don't take a lot of notice of most the men around here. Don't know why I noticed him so much. He just looked somehow out of place. Like he was that bit better than everyone else; and a little bit of him knew it.

They managed to get Tony onto the stretcher, and with some effort they carted him off to the medical tent for some well needed recuperation in the shade. I noticed a little tattoo on the medic'a right wrist, couldn't quite make out what it was, but it almost looked like a little snake wriggling down his arm. And just like that, they were all gone. The whole yard was empty, except for particles of sand being blown about like shopping bags. Maybe I should have helped them, but I couldn't get my legs to move in that heat. It also felt like a small part of me didn't want to be seen by the medic. Like if he saw me, he'd be better than me too. He probably was, you needed some brains about you to be a medic here, most had come here from medical school but needed something a little bit more exciting than sitting in a GPs office.

I finally managed to get my feet moving and moved over to one of the empty guard towers surround the perimeter of the camp. Only a few of them were manned at the moment because the threat was so low. I climbed to the top and rested my arms against the relative cool of the metal bars. Looking out across that fucking dessert, I couldn't help but think there must be more to this than standing around. When was I gonna be able to prove myself? When was I actually going to make a difference?

2

Des

Stupid bloody idiot, he'd been laying there for days. He was actually fine, but there was no convincing him of that, something about the isolation of the desert and that blow to the head had really set off a bout of hypochondria in him. Not that I suppose it mattered much; twenty beds in the med tent and all but one of them was empty. I suppose I should have been grateful for actually having something to do. There are only so many times I can clean the place and do check ups on the lads before people cotton on that I'm bored out of my brain.

I was sat there, looking through the medical histories of the guys for the millionth time, just trying to keep myself busy, it was about ten in the evening. There was a yellow glow coming from the floodlights dotted around the camp. How did end up there? I finished first in my class for my nursing degree, that should have been the end of it, I should have settled down and got a decent job in the city like Mum wanted. But no, there I was wasting my life in the middle of a desert surrounded by blokes with more muscles than brain cells.

I shouldn't be judgmental, they were trying to help, trying to do something good for queen and country and actually make an impact in the world. Hell, it's better than staying at home and living hand to mouth on minimum wage in some dead end job. There's not a lot for working class blokes like these to do back home except drive some lorries or labour on some worksite.

I picked up the black biro and gently nibbled at the plastic tip, pushing myself into a gentle tension with the chair. Another hour until my shift ended then I could crawl back to the tent, stroke myself off and get some sleep.

"Alright mate, how's the head?"

I spun around to see one of the goons from the football game poking his head through the green canvas of the tent. Sam I think his name was.

"Not good man, I reckon I've got concussion." Tony replied.

"How can you tell?"

"I'm just really groggy and slow."

"You're always like that!" Sam giggled like a bear and slapped Tony's arm. I rolled my eyes and pretended to be interested in the papers in front of me. I lifted the lid from the biro and started to doodle a small pattern in the corner of one of the soldiers' profiles. As I did that Sam leaned in and whispered into Tony's ear. I couldn't hear what was said but a chuckle spat from both of their mouths and Sam pulled away.

"Alright doc?" Sam offered.

"I'm not a Doctor."

"Listen, we're having some drinks over in rec later. Wanna join?"

"I've got lots of work to do."

"Oh yeah, busy healing all the sick?"

"He's a regular Jesus of Nazareth." Tony bellowed.

Sam rose from his position on Tony's bed and stumbled over to me. He had a weird glint in his eye and his teeth were gently growling at me.

"You're a pretty boy to find yourself out in the desert alone." He said, "I'm surprised mummy let you out."

I neglected to respond - I simply met his stare and attempted to hide the tremor in my hand. What sick game was he playing now? It seemed like he was flirting with me, but I'd been hit on by too many straight guys pissing about to take it seriously. All these tribal power plays drove me up the wall. All this testosterone left to itself to fester in the desert and we suddenly revert to pack animals. He was clearly scoping me out, seeing if I was a part of the pack or on the weak ones to be picked off.

"Oh pretty boy, don't worry, we'll look after you won't we Tone?"

"Hey, watch it man, he's been good to me in here." Tony responded.

"I'm fine looking after myself thanks."

He paused for a moment at the comment, glancing at me through the still of the evening with a slightly tilted head. The tattoos on his neck stretching and distorting as his shoulders muscles seemed to flex. His fist tightened and swung. For an instant my heart stopped and every muscle in my body froze. Then his hand grabbed my arm with some force and he stared into my eyes.

"Thanks for looking after Tony. He's a fucking idiot, I know, but he's not bad. Seriously doc, come have a drink.”

“I’m not a doctor.”

“Alright man! This ones hilarious tone! Got absolutely no sense of humour, but at least he’s looked after you. Listen, snap the fuck out of it and come down to rec. You’ve been in here days, to don’t need to stay. Kev’s got some beers and some draw.”

“You are free to go if you want Tony. You could have gone days ago.”

“But everything still feels a bit hazy…”

“Don’t be a fucking pussy tone.” Sam grabbed Tony’s arm and dragged him to his feet. “Come on mate, Ive got just the thing to sort you out.” As they were leaving Sam snuck a grin back at me over his shoulder. He had a look in his eye I couldn’t quite place. But when he was finally out of my sight I felt a big tension lift in my gut, there was something about him that unsettled me. Like I was never quite sure what he was thinking or what he was going to do next.

I felt so fucking alone there, miles from home, from my friends, from my family. All I wanted to do was sit with a bottle of wine and chat with a mate about how my day had gone. Maybe I should have gone to join the guys in rec. I didn’t really have any mates there. I kept myself to myself and just got on with the business of keeping the med tent moving. Which in all honesty didn’t take much.

When I started my placement, I was told to expect many casualties. The local militia group that had set up an outpost nearby were reportedly very aggressive. They had intercepted a shipment of munitions and were now armed to the teeth. I never had any interest in being the one in the line of fire, but if I could in any way help the guys brave enough to put themselves in the firing line. Then I had to do it. It wasn’t my plan to be here, but here I am - and I plan to do the best job I can while I’m here.

3

Kevin

There we were, sweating our bollocks off in the briefing tent. Lieutenant Mason called us in, no-one has any ideas why. Most of us were hanging out of our arseholes, we'd spent most of the last night drinking way too much and lighting each other's farts. Clearly way too much fun to be had out here in the field of battle.

"What the bloody hell are we here for?" Sam spat in my right ear, "my head is fucking killing mate. If they send us out in the field today I'll be more likely to spew on someone than shoot them."

"Don't worry mate, if you're not feeling too good I'm sure they'll let you cuddle up in bed with your teddy bear."

"Fuck off you dickhead."

Sam's head was dripping with little beads of sweat. He'd gone hard last night, I was surprised he was still standing. I wasn't quite sure how Sam had ended up there. We hadn't really spoken much about our pasts, we hadn't really spoken much about anything that actually mattered. We just drank and made crass jokes all the time. He had said something about having a little girl back home once. But I guess that can't have ended well or he wouldn't be here. If I had a kid waiting for me back at home there's no way I'd be here.

I'd much rather have a family and a life than be in this hell hole. But at the same time the thought of settling down with some bird makes me feel sick to the stomach. I'm too bloody young for that kinda shit. I need to do something with my life first. I'll work out what at some point. For now, I need to focus on surviving this.

I hear the door to the tent open behind us and in marches Mason looking stern as a cactus. 'He looks like an angry hedgehog' I thought to myself. Mason's got this weird way of talking sometimes. You can tell he doesn't want to say things, he always tries to hide whatever he's thinking and that means that when he opens his mouth he talks too much.

He made his way to the front of the tent, keeping his face completely still except for a slight twitching of his cheek betraying his nervousness. A uni education will get you into a position of authority quicker, but it won't make you any better at it. It takes a certain type of person to hold such power over others.

"Good morning boys." Mason finally spoke. "I hear you had a bit of a rough time last night. I hope you're not suffering too much. But we've got some work to do, things have been pretty quiet since we've been here. The rogue militia group that were allegedly in the area have been nowhere to be seen. But we think we've got some intel."

Mason went on to explain how the intel had come in from an Iraqi patrol that had run across them on their patrol. They'd found a house that had caught fire and the people inside were dead. Their bodies had burnt beyond recognition. There were several witnesses who had seen someone running away through the trees.

The militia group had apparently been putting pressure on the locals trying to gather support and intimidate them into following their rule. They want to set up their religious state and they'll wage holy war to get it.

The plan was to head into the village that had been attacked and see if we could see any signs of where the group were hiding.

This was it, we were finally going to get some action. Finally going to get into the line of fire. Now that the moment was here I felt a moment of fear. How would it actually feel to have a gun pointing at me? To have a bullet fired towards me. My stomach sank for a moment and then a shot of adrenaline and excitement spiked through me. I felt sick, but alive.

I looked around the tent and noticed that medic standing with his arms crossed by the door on my left. Again I felt this weird attraction towards him. I couldn't help but stare and felt curious as to what was going on in his head.

His expression seemed worried. For me the danger was getting shot, but he'd be the one trying to save my life. I can't imagine how it must feel to have that pressure. To be the one everyone looks to when they are in their worst state. When they are dying. I didn't want him to have to deal with that. For some reason I felt like I wanted to protect him. Like somehow I had already lost him. Whatever that meant.

My attention was pulled back to what Mason was saying.

"Okay so this mission starts tomorrow afternoon. If you think you can take care of yourselves, we're leaving as soon as we finish breakfast.

Good luck you guys, remember you aren't alone." Mason looked more scared than anyone, but was desperate to exude confidence.

After Mason had walked to his office, everyone started talking and laughing nervously. It wasn't a comfortable atmosphere; everyone knew the next few days were going to be dangerous as hell.

Everyone else headed out except for the medic who stood still, seemingly lost in his thoughts staring out of the tent towards the dusty horizon.   After a short while, he turned and slowly walked in my direction. He made eye contact with me as he tried to walk past, then he stopped.

"Are you coming with us?" He asked softly.

"Yeah, I am."

"Well, don't worry. You seem pretty capable."

He nodded and smiled slightly before turning and walking away. Then Sam grabbed me and pulled me out of the tent in a fit of testosterone induced excitement. This was it. I was finally going to do something with my life. Finally going to live.

4

Kevin

Everything was so yellow, and hot. Driving along in the midday sun, nothing but dry dust circling all around us for miles. I felt like I'd get sucked into it at any moment. Like the desolation would sense me and drink me up. I wouldn't want to get stuck out there alone, I count myself as pretty tough. But I don't think I'd last long in this environment.

It was mostly flat, but stretching out into the distance were the hills and moments, glaring yellow in the sun. That's where we were headed, apparently this village we were looking for was tucked away in the mountains.

The medic was sat opposite me in the truck. I'd spoken to Sam and apparently he was called Des. He was from London, had trained as a nurse and he was out here to get some more experience. He always looked like he was somewhere else. Something else on his mind. Like he had some really big problem he was trying to work out and the stuff going on around him was just trivial and incidental. Maybe it was.

He caught me looking at him, his brown eyes cut into me. They weren't particularly kind. But something in me was so drawn to him. I don't know what that was about. I looked away.

We'd never even had a conversation. Those words he said in the tent to me yesterday were the first I'd heard him utter. Why was I so interested in him?

"C'mon boys! Dont look so glum. Might be the last day we ever have." Sam piped up snarkily.

No-one really knew how to respond to that. Everyone had been so excited to be sent out, but now we were out here on the road there was a tension in the air that no one wanted to mention, but everyone could feel.

Time trundled on as well all sat there in silence. The air changed slightly as the truck entered the mountain path.

"You look worried." I looked around to see who was talking and saw Des staring at me expectantly.

"I'm fine, just getting myself in the zone I suppose." I replied.

"He's shitting himself." Sam said, "He's never seen any action before."

"Neither have you you nob-head."

"Oh, I've seen plenty of action." he responded while grabbing his crotch and squeezing.

The truck came to an abrupt stop.

Everything was quiet, I looked out the window and saw that we'd made it to the village. It seemed almost abandoned. there weren't many people about.

We jumped out of the truck. Everyone began to congregate at the front, all gathering round to look at something. Someone was sprawled out on the dirt road.

It looked like an elderly man by the looks of his hair. Des went over and tried to open his eyes and check his pulse, when out of nowhere he shot upright and began shouting at us. We couldn't understand a word, but someone translated for us.

"I said where are my kids?! Where did you take them?!" he said. "You bastards, you killed my kids!"

I tried speaking, "What happened to your kids, Sir?". The soldier translated, but it was no good. He kept yelling at me until I gave up trying to communicate with him.

Eventually he seemed to get exhausted in his mania and his breathing began to slow. He leant back in his arms and his screaming stopped.

The town was eerily quiet. The tension in the air was mad. No-one knew what to do, but we all felt that something was wrong.

"Where are my children, you son of a bitch?! What did you do to them?" He began to weep, staring intensely into my eyes and I could barely understand what he was saying.

One of the soldiers we were with, called Tom, started to get a bit edgy. I could see him reaching for his gun in a panic. I tried to signal to him that it was okay.

"Sir, please calm down." I said to him. "We're here to help. Please believe us. We don't know what has happened to your family."

I could see his face slowly calming as the soldier translated what I had said. Eventually he stopped and pointed slowly up towards to mountains. I looked where his finger was pointing and then found myself exchanging glances with Des.

Des looked back at me with a look of concern. I was scared, but something about having him there with me made me feel calm. What was he doing to me? No one had ever made me feel like that before.

There was nothing obvious in the direction that the old man had pointed. But that must have been the direction that the Militia went in. They'd clearly come in and taken some locals as hostage to draw us in. We needed to investigate but I couldn't help feeling that something wasn't right.

"Great, just a bunch of panicked locals. Still no action. He's clearly gone mad." Sam was kicking his feet in the dirt and grinning.

Des didn't say anything, instead he stared at the horizon. There was something about that look on his face that worried me. It wasn't like any look Des had given me before. His eyebrows knotted together in concentration, his mouth pressed tight into a thin line.

"Something's wrong." he said.

Before I could reply, a gunshot rang out through the valley. Everyone froze.

There was a moment of silence as everyone listened closely trying to work out where it had come from and what we should do. It was hard to tell what direction sounds came from because of the echo of The Valley.

My breath caught in my throat as another gunshot fired and a soldier standing screamed as a bullet shot into his arm. Blood splattering.

Everyone scattered, running in different directions. I ran towards some shrubbery on the mountainside to get some cover. Then another shot rang out and I felt something cutting through my leg. I stumbled and fell. This was it.

5

Gunshots were firing everywhere, and everyone was running in different directions. It was an ambush and all our training seemed to go out the window. As I was running towards shelter I saw Kevin fall the the ground. Blood pouring out of his leg.

I had to help him.

I ran over and hauled him up onto my shoulder. He was wincing and could barely stand, he didn't seem to be too aware of me. He just knew someone was there and something was happening.

There was a little ridge and some shrubbery just a few meters up ahead. I had to get us both to shelter or we'd both end up getting shot.

I started picking my way up the slope. Kevin hanging onto me for dear life, limping.

Another shot rang out from further up. I looked around frantically trying to find the shooter. A bullet whizzed past me, making me flinch.

The next thing I knew Kevin had grabbed a pistol from his side and shot our attacker. A militiaman who was hiding on the ridge further up. Kevin managed to shoot him straight in the face. He grabbed at himself, then collapsed and rolled down the hill.

He could barely walk but he was able to make a shot like that? I had no idea how he did it, but I was definitely impressed. I could feel the strong grip of his hand on my shoulder. This guy was capable.

We finally made it to the ridge and collapsed simultaneously behind some shrubs.

"Just wait here." I said, "We need to close up this wound."

I grabbed at his leg, which was pissing blood. The sounds of gunfire and shouts echoing through the village down below. I grabbed for my medpack for something to stop the flow of blood. If he kept bleeding at this rate he wouldn't last.

"I'm sorry." He said.

"You're fine. You're gonna be fine." I could see him slowly losing consciousness. I managed to clean the wound and get a basic bandage on there to stem the bleeding. I was sat holding pressure on the wound, trying to keep one eye on the surroundings. It didn't seem like anyone had noticed us slipping away.

Then I noticed a small opening further up the ridge and tucked away. Was it a cave? God I hoped it was a cave. If we could get in there I could get him safe and treat him properly.

"Kevin, stay awake. You're doing great. We just need to move a bit further and then you can relax." I said.

"The others." he croaked.

"There's nothing we can do right now. It was an ambush. Everyone is scattered." I looked into his eyes to try and reassure him. My blood was thrumming.

Everything was so much faster than usual, and every second we spent sitting here, the more in danger we were.

As if on cue, I heard some shouting coming from the valley below.

We looked out to see what the commotion was.

The village was full of militia. They were searching nearby buildings. Our forces were nowhere to be seen. Looks like everyone managed to get away without casualties. But there would definitely be plenty wounded. Everything had settled.

"Move." I whispered. "Now."

We moved slowly and quietly keeping as low to the ground as we could and using the ridge as cover as we scaled up the hill.

"Nearly there." I gasped into his ear.

Finally we collapsed into the cave and felt the cool of the air wrap around us. I closed my eyes and took a couple breaths in and out to steady my breathing.

When I opened my eyes I could see that   Kevins's face was still pale and sweating from the fight and blood loss. He looked exhausted but alive.

He reached for my hands and held them tightly.

"Thanks...for saving me back there." His words were slurred.

"Don't worry about it. That's my job. Just try and stay awake okay?"

I squeezed his hand.

His fingers were weak but I could feel their warmth and they were shaking against mine.

And he smiled faintly at me.

We were safe for now, but I needed to treat that wound properly or it would get infected. I unwrapped the bandages so I could clean it up properly and stop the bleeding. If possible, I needed to try and get the bullet out.

I unwrapped the bandages and saw the blood spilling out of his leg. It wasn't the time, but I couldn't help notice his lips. Even though he was struggling they looked so plump and kissable. And when I looked into those eyes, I realized that it was almost too late.

"Stay awake Kevin. Just stay awake.

Des

It was the middle of the night. We'd been stuck in the cave for about six hours now hiding from the Militia. I had no idea if they were still out there or not.

I sat at the edge of our makeshift bed looking out of the cave opening at the stars. I tried not to think about all the other men who were probably making their way through the desert on foot or holed up in caves like us. I hoped no one was captured.

I don't even know if they made it. We barely made it. I had managed to get the bullet out and Kevin seemed stable for now. But somehow I needed to get him back to camp for some proper medical attention. The wound could be infected and we'd need antibiotics.

All I know is that we needed to get out of there. Before things turned worse. Kevin laying sleeping behind me. He looked kind of gorgeous, even when he was ill like this.

Ever since I first saw him at the camp I thought he was really attractive. A bit rough for sure with his skinhead. You could tell life hadn't been kind to him, but there was a real warmth to him. It always amazed me how much kindness could be in someone that was tough all the time.

I don't know why I was thinking like that, he was clearly straight and this wasn't exactly the environment for starting a relationship with someone. We were in a war zone for Christ sake. I tried to shake the thoughts from my head but couldn't stop myself wondering what lay below the waist band of his trousers. I don't know how I was thinking about sex at a time like this. Something about the extreme danger just made me long for some physical affection.

How the hell did I end up here? I could be in a cushy hospital in London with plenty of men around to keep me warm at night. But here I was, risking my life in the middle of the desert. What was I thinking? I didn't know. But somehow I felt alive despite the fear.

There was a sense of freedom in doing whatever it takes to live.

Kevin began to stir, he was sweating and seemed a bit delirious. He started mumbling something and then he grabbed my wrist.

"Des?" he said. He couldn't open his eyes properly.

"I'm here mate, don't worry."

"I need…" he looked distraught, he wasn't thinking straight. Then ge started to cry. "I just wanted some love. That's all I wanted."

I didn't know what to say. People said all sorts of things when they were ill and delirious.

"Please…" He said. Even looking pale and ill he was kind of beautiful. His lips looked so soft. I held his hand to let him know I was there. The cool of the cave beneath us. The darkness. He was just going through a bad time.

"Get some rest." I whispered.

Then he grabbed me behind my neck and pulled me close. Before I knew it his lips were pressing against mine. My gut exploded with excitement, he was strong even now. He opened his eyes and flashed the blue of his iris towards me. Then he let go and drifted off back into sleep.

God knows how he'd feel about that when he came round.

6

Kevin

My dreams were scattered, light flickering, I was falling, something stroking me, grasping. Sweat, skin on skin. I couldn't breath. Light was falling on my eyes and I slowly became aware of the hard ground beneath me.

My eyes opened. Everything was blurry and I felt like hell. There was a grinding pain in my leg. All I could see was a little bit of sunlight filtering through a hole in the distance.

Where am I? The last thing I remember was fighting off all the militia. They must have killed everyone else...

I struggled to sit up and felt the intense agony coursing through my body. My leg aching.

"Hey hey, easy. You've had a rough night." A voice came from beside me. Des was sitting above me, he was topless. The brown of his nipples looked inviting. Why was I thinking about his nipples? What was wrong with me? His dog tag was dangling in between his pecks, he was surprising muscular for a skinny guy. "You shouldn't be moving."

What happened to the others? Where is everyone? Is anybody alright? Are they hurt? Where are the others.

"Just lay down. I'm sure everyone is fine. You're going to make yourself sick again." he said.

I stared wide eyed at him. He's worried about me. Why? Why would he care?

Memories were flashing through my mind. Gunfire, climbing the hill, a bullet ripping through me. Then I remembered his lips. Did he kiss me? Was it a dream?

Did we actually do that? Am I dying? Am I in heaven? Oh god, did

I die? Please don't let me die. Don't leave me alone.

Des grabbed my hand.

"Come on. Stay still."

He laid me back down gently. "Try and relax okay? Try and sleep some more."

He was leaning over me. His warm breath brushed against my lips. I swallowed heavily and licked them as I felt a tingling sensation spread over my body. I could feel my cheeks burning. Why was I blushing? This wasn't good. I had to focus on anything but him. Focus on breathing.

The sun had risen high in the sky and bright rays of sunshine falling into the cave we were in.

Then came the sound of scrambling and a whimper of pain from outside. Both of us froze. Someone was out there. We stayed there a moment and listened for more, his hand resting on my abdomen. Then there was a muffled groaning.

"Wait here. I need to check that out." He said. He rose and slowly exited the entrance of the cave. He was gone a few minutes leaving me laying there trying to get my mind straight. There was so much pain running through me yet somehow I felt horny. I could feel blood trying to pump into my cock. My balls covered in sweat and sticking to my thighs. What I wouldn't give for a good hard fuck right now. I wanted my cock in someone. Now.

I tried to get the though from my mind. This was a war zone not some sex club. But clearly something about fighting for my life made the adrenaline pulse through me like some twisted aphrodisiac.

I don't know how long he was gone, but when he came back through the cave entrance there was someone else hanging off of his shoulder. I couldn't make out there faces with the sunlight shining in behind them. The person looked familiar but I couldn't place them.

Des lowered the person to the ground and he stumbled forward towards me. I noticed his chest rising and falling fast, sweat beading at his brow.

Then suddenly he fell forward onto the rock floor. It was Sam! I'd recognise that skin head anywhere.

"Alright boys?" he said, straining. He was clearly in a lot of pain.

"Sam." The word managed to leave my mouth.

"We're fucked. I thought I was the only one left. Everyone else was taken out, I think maybe some boys were taken prisoner. We're absolutely fucked."

"We need to find a way back to the camp." Des said.

"No fucking kidding. But we can't, we're in their territory and we're completely outnumbered."

"Are they still out there?"

"I don't know. I've been hiding all night trying to stay out of sight."

"Surely they wouldn't stick around. I need to go out and check the area. It's the only option, we can't stay here with no food and no water."

"It's not safe." I said. "You can't go out there alone."

"There's no other option. You two are in no condition. We can't stay here or we really are fucked. Thanks for your concern though." He flashed me a smile and my stomach flipped. What was happening to me? Being out here was making my body do crazy things. I'd never been attracted to a guy before and suddenly all I could think about was Des's mouth around my balls, sucking off all the sweat.

I didn't want him to go out there on his own. But there was nothing I could do. I could feel a hard on forming in my pants. How was I this horny? I was in danger and all I could think about was cumming over his face.

"You guys stay here. I won't be long. I just need to scout and see if the militia are still in the area." Des said as he made his way out of the cave.

Then Sam and I were left in the cave, both of us weak, sweating leaning on the cool cave floor for support. Sam was looking at me, he looked defeated, he looked lost.

"This isn't gonna end well mate. We're done for." Sam said.

"We'll be fine Sam. Des knows what he's doing."

"Alright gay boy. Your boyfriend gonna sort everything out?"

"Fuck off Sam! We're out here alone. We've got to find a way to work together."

"I know we're alone! As soon as the gunshots started everyone scattered. They all abandoned us, all that talk of brotherhood suddenly meant nothing." We were both angry. We were both scared.

Sam was panting in his frustration, then his eyes seemed to rest on something. He was staring intently, what was that look? Embarrasment? I looked in the direction of his eyes.

Fuck.

My cock was rock hard, you could see it through my trousers, throbbing.

He was staring at it, then he was looking at me. A weird grin on his face. "I guess the fear of death does different things to everybody." He chuckled.

"My body doesn't know what it's doing. I'm all over the place mate."

"Me too." He said as he looked away. Then he looked back towards my cock and tilted his head. "Well, it would be a shame to die without ever cumming again."

"Not exactly much of an option out here. Unless you know a good club nearby?" I let out an awkward laugh. Then something happened that I never thought I'd see. Sam moved over towards me and began stroking his hand along my trousers, pressing his palm into my cock.

"We can work something out mate. What else are friends for?" and with that he began rubbing a little faster up and down my cock through the fabric. Gripping onto my shaft.

I'd never been wanked off by a bloke before, let alone in a cave in the middle of a desert with a bullet hole in my stomach. But god, I can't lie, it felt fucking good to feel some pleasure. The blood pumped into my rod even harder, the skin rubbing against my underwear. Precum sticking to the fabric.

After a few moments, he checked that I was enjoying it and then unzipped my trousers and pulled my cock out from the underwear.

There it was, my hard rod standing to attention. Sam's hand wrapped around it. He smiled then began stroking up and down me. I couldn't help but let out a moan. It was weird, but it felt so fucking good. My foreskin sliding up and down over my bellend.

I couldn't resist any longer and began thrusting my hips upwards, moaning with every movement. He laughed softly then continued. Stroking my cock with his finger, slowly rolling his knuckle across the top of my sac. It felt amazing. I started thrashing and moaning louder.

He was really picking up some speed.

"Oh Jesus Christ, Sam. I'm going to cum." I yelled.

"That's the spirit buddy, keep going."

He was pumping harder and faster now. My cock began to twitch and throb. I wanted to come so bad. God help me, I wanted to come.

"Faster Sam." I moaned.

"Yeah, yeah. Just a bit longer."

"Please."

"Almost there."

"Yes." I moaned, staring at the ceiling of the cave. The rock pushing into the soft cheeks of my ass. The rock was cold against my skin, the cave air cooling my hot sweaty body.

I needed more. Then it arrived.

Fire spread through my body and hot cum spurted out of cocking spreading itself all over Sam's hands and my torso. White ribbons spattering everywhere. I felt my muscles tense and release and forgot everything about where I was and what was going on.

There was silence as I started to return to normal consciousness and Sam slowly let go of my cock.

"Well someone is feeling better." It was Des. I looked up and there he was standing at the cave entrance. A grin over his face as he stood staring at me, covered in cum.

7

Des

There was Kevin, covered in his own cum. Sam's hand covered too. What had I missed? I wanted to be angry, but I couldn't lie. Seeing Kevin Laying there, strings of white over his six pack, beads of sweat over his pecks and forehead. He looked fucking hot and I couldn't believe I didn't make it there a few minutes before.

They were both looking at me awkwardly, not knowing what to say. I could see Sam's boner poking through his trousers and mine was on its way.

"Our lives are at risk you know." I said.

"Exactly, who wants to die horny?" Sam replied. Kevin just stared at me looking embarrassed. He looked really sweet, like he'd done something wrong. I guess these two didn't know I was gay, this type of thing didn't phase me at all. In fact part of me was a bit disappointed that I hadn't seen more of this in the army. I had had all sorts of stupid fantasies before leaving. Not wanting to admit it even to myself, I had always been kind of turned on by the military life. Now I knew it must have been hormones messing with me but still I found myself wondering how long it would take before I was able to get a dick inside me.

The three of us stayed silent. A weird tension in the air. Sam coughed, finally deciding to break the quiet.

"So uh…any luck out there?"

"I managed to sneak down to the truck. It seems like the militia have scrambled. I radioed back to base and they're going to send out a resume helicopter ASAP. Shouldn't be long maybe a couple of hours."

"Were there any other survivors down there?"

"I couldn't see anyone."

"Looks like we'll just have to hang tight then." Kevin said.

The air was awkward. It was filled with relief, fear, grief, but somehow, amongst all of this I could feel Sam's blood pumping - and mine too. The sight of Kevin still covered in cum was too much for me to cope with.

Sam tentavely leant backwards and rubbed at his cock through his trousers. "Listen boys, I know this is a weird situation. But do you mind if I finish myself off?"

Kevin looked at him for a moment. Then he laughed nervously and nodded. He was trying to hide his erection.

"If you want that." Kevin said.

Sam grinned and pulled himself free of his trousers. He looked at me with a smirk. "Don't worry mate. You can join in if you want."

I didn't really know how to react. I didn't much like Sam, he was irritating and loud. And this wasn't really the right place to be getting my rocks off. But Kevin had done it and something about knowing we were going to be safe did make me feel more relaxed. I could do with taking my mind off of this hell.

Sam lay himself on the ground and began beating his meat, letting a little moan come out. Kevin's cock began to harden again and mine was throbbing too. This was insane.

Desperate times call for desperate measures. I removed my trousers. The sight of Sam stroking himself made me groan as I crawled over to him. His cock pulsating in his hand.

I lay down in between him and Kevin and pulled my underwear down over my cock. All three of us lay there stroking our cocks and moaning.

I couldn't help but look at Kevin lying next to me. He really did look handsome. The sight of his cock bouncing in between his knuckles was too much for me.

So I took the opportunity to stroke myself up and down, which was difficult when Sam and Kevin had me sandwiched between them, Sam's large balls grazing my side.

My balls began to tighten as I increased my strokes. The heat was intense and I was starting to feel weak.

Kevin was grinning at me. Then he whispered in my ear, "I've been dreaming about this."

I couldn't believe it. Kevin had been fantasising about me? Well I wasn't expecting that, but it turned me on even more. I let my other hand slip down between my legs as my finger started to play with my puckered ass. I bit down on my bottom lip as I let out an involuntary moan.

Kevin rolled over and leaned into me as I slipped my finger inside myself letting my legs spread. His lips almost touching my ear. "Can I fuck you?" He asked.

I looked over to my right to see Sam beating away at himself and moaning. Kevin's heat was intoxicating and I wanted so badly for him to fuck me. I wanted him to fuck me blind on that cave floor and cum inside me.

"I want your dick." I replied. Somehow he found the strength to move above me. The hole in his leg didn't seem to bother him. Maybe it wasn't infected after all.

He flipped me onto my front. And pushed his tongue in between my cheeks. It felt so good to have him licking inside my asshole. All I could do was moan and watch Sam next to me who was watching the events before him with glee.

"Go on boys." He said, clearly up for watching what eve show was about to take place.

Kevin slid one finger into me and moved it around slowly. My hips began rocking rhythmically towards him. He grabbed my hip with his other hand and slowly let me fuck his finger.

A second later I was crying out in pleasure as Kevin pushed another finger in and began pounding his thumb against my prostate.

I felt my orgasm building inside of me, but still I tried to hold back and not let myself go. "I need to cum!" I growled.

"You're gonna have to wait. I want my cock in you. I've been dying to fuck you ever since we got to this cave." Kevin said.

"Yeah, fuck his boy pussy." Sam snarled as he slapped my ass and got up on his knees,

still stroking himself.

"With pleasure."

"You're gonna need plenty of spit. Unfortunately I didn't pack lube." I giggled.

Kevin

I was letting dollops of my spit slip over his wrinkled little asshole as I slid my finger in and out making his hole as wet as I could. He moaned and bucked upwards as I kept pushing myself in deeper.

The more he moved his body, the faster I fucked him with my fingers. The smell of his ass filling the air. Sam was next to me wanking himself, grunting and slapping Des's perky brown ass. I was so turned on that the pain in my leg had evaporated into nothing.

I was ready to push my cock inside him.

"You ready?" I asked.

"Fuck him." Sam jumped in. "Fuck him like a whore."

And with that I rested my dick on his opening and began to push into Kevin's ass, stretching him as far as I could. I felt his lips open for me, there was a little bit of friction. Spit wasn't the perfect lube. But it was good enough.

"Oh my god!" He cried out.   "Shit! Fuck. Oh shit! That feels so good."

I pushed into his ass as far as I could while pulling his hips closer to me. We both gasped for air and Sam was panting heavily next to us.

"Shit this feels good!" I gasped.

"You fucking freak. Fuckin freak." Sam chuckled. "Fuck him Kev. Make him scream."

I let my hips grind harder into his, feeling my body growing tighter. With every thrust Des was moaning louder. His hole was so warm and tight and inviting. I felt better than I ever had in my life. I could feel my bellend rubbing up against his prostate. Bareback meant I could feel every inch of his asshole as I pushed into him.

"Faster! Faster! Fuuuck! Fuck!" Sam screamed. "Come for me Kev! Cum inside his hole."

I was losing it. I could feel my balls becoming sore from all the movement I was doing. Des was whimpering as I slammed into his cheeks. I could feel myself getting close again.

"Come! Come for me Kev! Fuck me now!" Des screamed.

I felt my seed start to leak into his hole as I started to thrust harder into his ass. The pain in my leg began to fade as I felt the warmth of my seed getting ready to shoot. I could feel myself beginning to climax inside him.

Then I fired my load, filling up Des's tight passage. The pressure was immense.

I continued to fuck Des, filling him with every last drop of me as he cried out and screamed. His face was screwed up into such an ugly expression and as he came on the cave floor.

A few seconds later and Sam was grunting, spraying his cum all over Des's ass. White streaks licking across the brown of those sweet cheeks as I continued to move slowly in and out of him.

I collapsed forward against Des's back, breathing hard. My legs shook and trembled. I could hardly keep upright anymore.

"That was amazing!" Des spoke.   He didn't seem bothered that my cum was dripping out of his ass. In fact he seemed delighted. "Thank you for that."

I felt a smile form on my face. "Thanks…" I managed to say.

Sam laughed and watched me as I pulled out of Des with a groan and we all collapsed in a sweaty cum covered heap on the floor. Limbs draped over eachother.

"Let's keep this to us boys." Sam finally said with a laugh. "Don't want everyone knowing the secret to surviving out here." We all laughed. This was mad, there we were, fighting for our lives. And all we could think about was fucking each other. I guess life is a weird thing, and the thought of losing it is even weirder. It makes you realise what's really important. Friends, warmth, affection and a good fuck.

Epilogue

Kevin

We were in the evac helicopter, flying over the desert, sand pissing in through the window. Across from me sat Des and Sam, both of them looking my weirdly happy. I didn't know if they were happy because we'd escaped or happy because they'd got their ends away. Maybe both.

The rescue helicopter had taken a few hours to turn up. After we recovered from our first fuck we all had a wank together. It's like we were some strange brotherhood now and somehow finding pleasure in each other was a way to keep us going. Well, whatever had happened. It had worked, we were safe and we were headig back to base.

My leg didn't feel great, but Des has done a good job treating me. I was confident I'd recover pretty easily.

Des caught me looking at him and gave me a sneaky wink. He moved over next to me in the helicopter. I couldn't hear much because of the propellers, but he leaned closer to my ears to make sure I could hear.

"Thanks for everything Kev. I was really glad to have you back there. That was the first time I've ever been in action. It was good to have a mate there."

"Don't worry about it." I replied. "You saved my life. I should be thanking you."

"Well, what happened in the cave earlier was a good start." He grinned at me knowingly. Oh I see. He was hoping we'd do that again? I didn't know how to felel about that. I didn't see myself as gay. But then again, the thought of having my cock inside him again did sound good.

The thing was I didn't really want to just have sex. I wanted to build something a bit deeper with someone. I'd never thought of doing that with a guy before. But Des seemed special. Maybe I had to let go of labels like straight and gay and just spend time with someone I was attracted to. Who knew what the future would bring?

"Well, I'm sure there will be other opportunists." I whispered back to him. Sam caught our eye and smiled knowingly. Gay or not, I had a feeling we'd be fucking again before long. Des was a good mate, and for whatever reason, he really did turn me on. And he did save my life. If he wanted me to fuck him as a reward then I guess I'd just have to go along with it. What's a man to do. And as for the rest, well, I guess we'd have to wait and see.

Excerpt From The Construction Worker

My feet were bloody killing me. Six o'clock in the morning and my mouth was as dry as Ghandi's flip flop. I'd just about managed to drag myself out of bed and was just slumping along the pavement hovering my hands over my head to shelter from the rain. Just my luck to turn up soaked for the first day.

My mate Ben had managed to get me the job on recommendation - he always managed to get me these last minute gigs. I was trying to get out of the labouring trade but there just seemed to be nothing else about at the moment. Nothing that I fancied anyway. I wanted something a bit better for myself, but somehow always ended up exactly back where I started wondering how I'd got there.

I could feel the wet of my T-shirt clinging to me, all white and heavy. It felt nice and fucking irritating all at the same time. Like a soggy hug from your best mate.

I'd thought about going to college and studying to be a chef or something. Catering, I think the course was called, but the course leader bloody hated me. Well, I say she hated me. I think she was more annoyed that I didn't fancy her. She was this fit forty odd year old woman. She really was fit, but I've never been able to keep it up for older women. I don't know why; just always feels like I'm shagging my mum - not ideal.

My trainers were slapping the wet pavements making drips of mud slip up my legs like tiny pieces of shit. To say I felt disgusting would be a complete understatement.

I got to the building site around quarter past six. Fifteen minutes late on the first day isn't too bad I suppose. I could blame delays on the tube or something; no-one would know any different.

I trampled onto the mud and gravel littering the ground at the entrance to the site. Big mesh gates shivering either side of me while the slap of the puddles fought against the patter of rain. Just to the right of the entrance stood a six foot security guard scowling inside his hut, giving me the eye through his half open window.

We exchanged a few words and he pointed me in the direction of a hut about twenty meters down the site.

I opened the door, pushing myself into the shelter of the blue grey sanctuary. A wave of heat met my wet skin and made me want to vomit. Either that or those vodka and cokes were repeating on me. I let the bile settle in my stomach, then turned to see a room full of blokes in high-vis, scattered around in various states of boredom.

"Dan?" A bald bloke with shoulders the size of dumbbells was walking over to me with a clipboard.

"For my sins." I shook out my jacket and pulled my hood down, letting myself drip all over the dirty laminate floor, "sorry I'm late."

"Don't worry, we're running late anyway. Fucking rain."

"Tell me about it." I signalled to the ocean sliding down my clothes.

"Grab a cuppa and dry off. I'll come get you when we work out where you'll be."

"Thanks mate."

I managed to get myself a hot drink and made my way to huddle over by the radiator at the far side of the room. I knew it'd be no hassle me being late. No way anyone's gonna get any work done today anyway; not unless that rain lets up - not likely.

I took off my jacket and hung it over the radiator. Leaving me stood there with my soaking wet T-shirt clinging to my chest, my tattoos starting to show through the fabric - it would dry eventually.

About ten minutes later and the bald bloke came back over to me, "You feeling dry?"

"As dry as I'm gonna get."

"Listen, don't think it's likely we're gonna have any work for you today."

I bristled for a moment, then came back with, "You what?"

"Sorry mate, not the day for it. Rain makes it unsafe."

"You're still gonna pay me?"

He paused a moment and looked over his shoulder with a twitch, "Sorry mate."

"Fucking ridiculous." I spat, "I could have had a days work elsewhere! I lose a days money cause your lot can't handle the rain."

"Alright mate, calm down."

I grabbed my jacket and slid it on to me, feeling the damp scrape across my arms, "Oh yeah, calm down. I'll do that, mate, yeah. Just cozy up in my penthouse with some champagne and calm down, I will."

I made my way out through the door and back in the torrential rain still hammering onto the brown grey of the ground. Couldn't fucking believe it, Ben always managed to set me up with these bullshit gigs.

What type of dickheads don't pay after dragging me all the way down here at the crack of dawn?

I had no idea what to do with myself when I got out of the building site and back onto the pavement. Managed to huddle myself under a red awning from the nearby off-license. The smell of day old fruit and veg mingling with the rain. My life was really going well.

I hope you enjoyed the book!
I'm an independent author so your feedback is really valuable. Please leave a review if you can or feel free to drop me some personal feedback to: tomnorthauthor@gmail.com
If you would like to sign-up to my mailing list for offers and news on future releases please follow the link:
https://mailchi.mp/1613c8979d1a/tom-north-narratotr
Thanks for reading!
Xx